# Note to parents, carers and teachers

*Read it yourself* is a series of modern stories, favourite characters and traditional tales written in a simple way for children who are learning to read. The books can be read independently or as part of a guided reading session.

Each book is carefully structured to include many high-frequency words vital for first reading. The sentences on each page are supported closely by pictures to help with understanding, and to offer lively details to talk about.

The books are graded into four levels that progressively introduce wider vocabulary and longer stories as a reader's ability and confidence grows.

## Ideas for use

- Begin by looking through the book and talking about the pictures. Has your child heard this story before?

- Help your child with any words he does not know, either by helping him to sound them out or supplying them yourself.

- Developing readers can be concentrating so hard on the words that they sometimes don't fully grasp the meaning of what they're reading. Answering the puzzle questions at the end of the book will help with understanding.

*For more information and advice on Read it yourself and book banding, visit* www.ladybird.com/readityourself

Book Band 5

**Level 1** is ideal for children who have received some initial reading instruction. Each story is told very simply, using a small number of frequently repeated words.

## Special features:

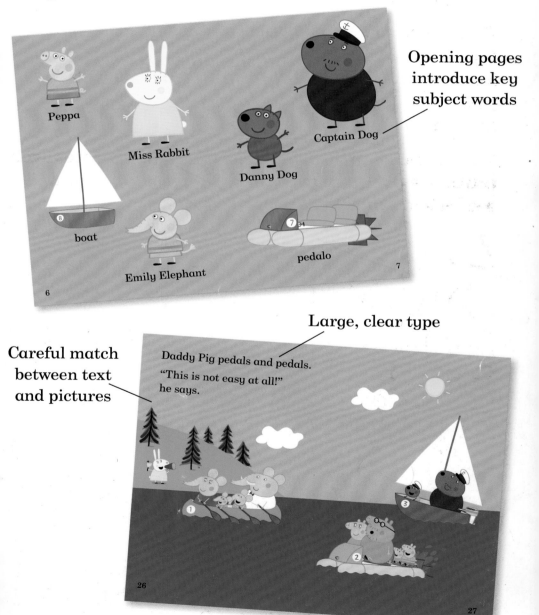

Opening pages introduce key subject words

Peppa

Miss Rabbit

Danny Dog

Captain Dog

boat

Emily Elephant

pedalo

6

7

Large, clear type

Careful match between text and pictures

Daddy Pig pedals and pedals.
"This is not easy at all!" he says.

26

27

# Educational Consultant: Geraldine Taylor
# Book Banding Consultant: Kate Ruttle

LADYBIRD BOOKS

UK | USA | Canada | Ireland | Australia
India | New Zealand | South Africa

Ladybird Books is part of the Penguin Random House group of companies
whose addresses can be found at global.penguinrandomhouse.com.

www.penguin.co.uk  www.puffin.co.uk  www.ladybird.co.uk

Text adapted from 'Peppa Goes Boating', first published by Ladybird Books, 2014
This edition first published by Ladybird Books, 2017
002

This book copyright © ABD Ltd/Ent. One UK Ltd 2017
Adapted by Ellen Philpott

This book is based on the
TV Series 'Peppa Pig'.
'Peppa Pig' is created by
Neville Astley and Mark Baker.
Peppa Pig © Astley Baker Davies Ltd/
Entertainment One UK Ltd 2003.

www.peppapig.com

Printed in China

A CIP catalogue record for this book is
available from the British Library

ISBN: 978-0-241-27971-7

All correspondence to
Ladybird Books
Penguin Random House Children's Books
80 Strand, London WC2R 0RL

# Going
# Boating

Peppa

Miss Rabbit

boat

Emily Elephant

Captain Dog

Danny Dog

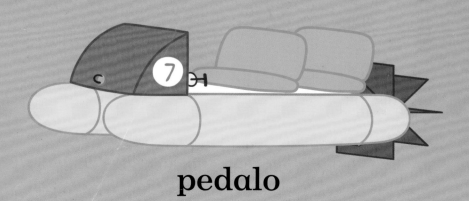

pedalo

Peppa and her family
are going boating.

"Boats! Come and get a boat here!" says Miss Rabbit.

"Not these boats," says
Daddy Pig. "We would like
one of the easy ones, please."

"These pedalos are easy," says Mummy Pig.

"I would like a pedalo, please," says Daddy Pig.

Peppa and her family all get into the pedalo.

"You will have to pedal!" says Miss Rabbit.

Emily Elephant and her family are going boating, too.

"We would like this one, please," says Daddy Elephant.

Danny Dog and Captain
Dog are going boating, too.

"We would like this one,
please," says Captain Dog.

Everyone is boating!

"You have to pedal, Daddy," says Peppa.

"This is not so easy,"
Daddy Pig says.

All of the boats are here.
It is time for a picnic.

Everyone loves picnics!

"Time to come in!" says
Miss Rabbit.

"So, who will get back first?"
says Mummy Pig.

Daddy Pig pedals and pedals.
"This is not easy at all!"
he says.

It is Captain Dog who gets back first.

"I love boating," he says.

# Everyone loves boating!

How much do you remember about the story of Peppa Pig: Going Boating? Answer these questions and find out!

- What kind of boat does Daddy Pig choose?

- Who else comes boating?

- Who is the first to get their boat back to Miss Rabbit?

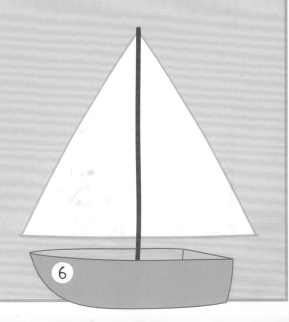

6

# Look at the pictures from the story and say the order they should go in.

A

B

C

D

# Tick the books you've read!

## Level 1

## Level 2